little ellen

Ellen DeGeneres

Illustrated by
Eleanor Michalka

Based on the television series *Little Ellen* created by Kevin A. Leman II

Random House
New York

It's Little Ellen here—
I'm seven years old!
What truly makes me *me*?
Not sure, truth be told.

Is it my **cool dance moves**?

(Which I bet
you can't do.)

Go ahead! Try some!

Oh. You do them, too. . . .

Perhaps it's the thoughts that **zoom** inside my mind:

Why's the cat got your tongue?

Who's this Nick of time?

Wait! Wait! I know the deal!

It's like nothing I've said—

me is my heart,

and not in my head.

Looking right here,
I find all that I love:

my Gramsy,

my friends,

my "World's Greatest Mug"!

When I think of these things,
my heart wants to burst.

Who **I** am is about
all of **those** I put first!

I guess that's the whole thing that makes me into **me**:

my big, generous heart that no one can see.

My heart's full of **colors**,
not because of myself.

No, it's all that I do
for everyone else.

My heart got its **sparkles**

when I saw someone crying

and then made them laugh.
It's just about trying!

My heart gets its **glow**
from the kind things I do.

I listen, speak up—
I'm **there** through and through.

My heart's got ladybugs, scooters, and fireflies inside!

There's a sweet little sloth
and a whole lot of pride.

So, always remember:
Take what you love;
hold it tight.

It'll color your heart
for the rest of your life.

You are **all** that you are,
all you can do.

Wow. So spectacular.
I'm so glad that you're **you**!

Copyright © 2022 by Ellen Digital Ventures
Jacket art and interior illustrations by Eleanor Michalka

All rights reserved. Published in the United States by Random House Children's Books,
a division of Penguin Random House LLC, New York.

Random House and the colophon are registered trademarks of
Penguin Random House LLC.

Visit us on the Web! rhcbooks.com

Educators and librarians, for a variety of teaching tools, visit us at
RHTeachersLibrarians.com

Library of Congress Cataloging-in-Publication Data is available upon request.
ISBN 978-0-593-37860-1 (trade) — ISBN 978-0-593-37861-8 (ebk)

The artist created the illustrations for this book digitally.
The text of this book is set in 17-point Ideal Sans.
Interior design by Nicole Gastonguay
MANUFACTURED IN CHINA
10 9 8 7 6 5 4 3 2 1
First Edition